JAIM

cows
are flying

COWS ARE FLYING

First edition. August 9, 2023.

ISBN: 979-8223051480

Written by Jaime Orozco.

Chapter 1: Udderly Unbelievable

In the quaint little town of Mooington, life was as tranquil as the gentle mooing of cows in a sun-dappled pasture. The townsfolk went about their routines, sipping coffee at the local café, tending to their gardens, and exchanging pleasantries as if they were characters from a Norman Rockwell painting.

But in Mooington, things were about to take a decidedly peculiar turn.

It was an ordinary Tuesday morning when Farmer Bob, the proud owner of the biggest dairy farm in town, stumbled upon a sight that defied all logic. He rubbed his eyes in disbelief and blinked at the sky. There, amidst the cotton candy clouds, floated a cow. A cow, mind you, with a rather bemused expression and a pair of wings flapping furiously.

"By all that's pasture-worthy!" Farmer Bob exclaimed, his jaw dropping. "The cows are flying!"

Word of this absurd spectacle spread like wildfire. Soon, the townspeople abandoned their chores and gathered at the town square, craning their necks to witness cows soaring through the sky with the grace of... well, cows.

Mayor Thompson, a portly man with a penchant for wearing bowties and making grand speeches, cleared his throat. "Ladies and gentlemen of Mooington, it appears that the impossible has happened. Cows, our four-legged friends and providers of creamy milk, have taken to the skies!"

Gasps and giggles filled the air as the townsfolk tried to make sense of the surreal sight. Cows with wings? It was the kind of thing that belonged in a comic book, not a quaint town that prided itself on a yearly "Best Cheese" competition.

As the day progressed, chaos ensued. Cows crash-landed in gardens, startled pigeons dodged clumsy cow fliers, and a particularly adventurous cow attempted to perform loop-de-loops, much to the bewilderment of onlookers.

By sunset, Mooington resembled a farmyard meets an aviation show. It was as if cows had decided to rewrite the laws of gravity in their bovine manifesto.

Meanwhile, Nancy Murphy, the town's quirky veterinarian, rolled up her sleeves and examined one of the flying cows, which had landed with a thud right outside her clinic.

"Well, I never thought I'd see the day," she muttered, examining the cow's wings with a mix of fascination and professional skepticism. "These wings seem genuine. Could it be some cosmic anomaly?"

Rumors swirled about extraterrestrial cow kidnappings and government experiments gone awry. Conspiracy theories were crafted and debunked with equal fervor, while the cows themselves continued their uncoordinated flights, causing a parade of absurd mishaps.

The next morning, Farmer Bob emerged from his barn, a determined look in his eyes. "We can't just stand here gawking at flying cows," he declared. "We need to get them down safely before someone gets trampled by a clumsy heifer."

A team of townsfolk armed with ladders, trampolines, and even makeshift cow-catching nets assembled beneath the floating cows. It was a sight to behold—mooing, laughter, and a chorus of exclamations filled the air as each cow was carefully and not-so-elegantly retrieved from the sky.

By the time the sun set, the town square was strewn with feathered bovine, and the townsfolk collapsed in exhaustion, a sense of camaraderie forming among them. The flying cows had turned Mooington into a community bound by a hilarious, if bizarre, shared experience.

As night settled in and the stars twinkled above, a sense of wonder lingered. What cosmic forces had conspired to turn everyday cows into airborne wonders? And what could possibly happen next in the zany tale of "The Cows Are Flying"?

Chapter 2: Bovine Aeronautics

The morning sun rose over Mooington, casting a warm glow on the town square where cows—now firmly grounded—were being tended to by a team of veterinarians and bemused farmers. It seemed that the flying episode had left the cows with a sense of newfound dignity, as if they were seasoned aviators recounting their daring escapades.

Nancy Murphy was hard at work, examining the wings of a particularly majestic Holstein named Daisy. "Well, Daisy, it appears you're quite the trendsetter," Nancy chuckled, giving the cow an affectionate pat.

Mayor Thompson stood beside a whiteboard, earnestly scratching his head. "Ladies and gentlemen, it's clear that our town has become the epicenter of an extraordinary phenomenon. The scientific community is abuzz with theories, and I'm sure a delegation of experts will arrive any moment now."

Indeed, as if on cue, a convoy of vehicles rumbled into town, adorned with logos of renowned scientific institutions. A team of researchers, each sporting various degrees of dishevelment, emerged with clipboards and measuring instruments.

Dr. Evelyn Wallace, a bespectacled scientist with a penchant for lab coats and rapid speech, took center stage. "Greetings, citizens of Mooington! We are here to unravel the mystery of your flying cows. Prepare for a barrage of experiments, hypotheses, and possibly a few moments of confusion."

The townsfolk watched as Dr. Wallace and her team scurried about, collecting samples, analyzing wing structures, and muttering scientific jargon that could have been mistaken for cow dialogue.

Farmer Bob leaned over to Nancy, a bemused grin on his face. "I never thought I'd see the day when scientists would be treating my cows like extraterrestrial visitors."

3

As the day unfolded, the scientists conducted a series of experiments that ranged from measuring the aerodynamic qualities of the cow wings to analyzing the cows' behavior before, during, and after their flights. It was, in essence, a study in bovine aeronautics.

By sunset, the town square had turned into a chaotic laboratory, cows and researchers mingling in a surreal symphony of science and barnyard charm. The townsfolk found themselves unwitting participants, answering questions about cow diets, daily routines, and even their dreams (or lack thereof).

That night, the townspeople gathered at the local diner to share stories and speculate on the odd occurrence. "Maybe it's a sign," mused Emily, a local schoolteacher known for her boundless optimism. "A sign that we should all aim high and spread our wings."

Laughter and agreement filled the air, and soon the diner buzzed with ideas for cow-themed inventions, from "Cow Air Shows" to "Milk-Propelled Rocketry."

Meanwhile, Mayor Thompson wrestled with his bowtie, deep in thought. "Perhaps we should embrace this strange turn of events and turn Mooington into a tourist destination. Imagine the slogans: 'Where Dreams Take Flight—And Cows Too!'"

The next day, Mooington's transformation began. Banners with cow-themed slogans adorned the streets, and the town square had transformed into a bovine-themed fairground. Visitors from neighboring towns arrived, eager to witness the flying cow phenomenon and sample the finest dairy products.

As the festivities kicked off, laughter and joy filled the air, and even the cows seemed to revel in the attention, donning makeshift aviator hats and basking in the spotlight. The townspeople had embraced the absurdity of their situation, turning it into a celebration of community and the unpredictable nature of life.

As night fell, the townsfolk gazed at the starlit sky, reminiscing about the flying cows and the unexpected turns life can take. The tale of "The

Cows Are Flying" had only just begun, leaving Mooington's inhabitants wondering what other bovine surprises the universe might have in store.

Chapter 3: A Herd of Dreams

Mooington had truly embraced its status as the town of flying cows. The bovine-themed fairground had become a lively attraction, complete with cow-shaped Ferris wheels, flying cow parades, and even a "Milkshake Mile" race that involved sprinting while balancing a milkshake on a tray.

Visitors flocked to the town, capturing photos of themselves with cows donning aviator goggles and grinning broadly. The local economy boomed as souvenir shops peddled cow-themed trinkets, and the dairy products became renowned for their "airborne authenticity."

Farmer Bob had a perpetual grin on his face as he interacted with visitors, regaling them with stories of his cows' soaring escapades. "You see, these cows are not just ordinary cows—they're dreamers who decided to chase the sky!"

Nancy Murphy had her hands full, tending not only to the health of the cows but also the countless tourists who occasionally tripped over their own excitement. She chuckled as she treated a tourist who had a sprained ankle, muttering something about "flying too close to the sun."

As the festivities continued, the sense of community in Mooington deepened. Neighbors became friends, and strangers became companions in the quest for the perfect cow selfie. The townspeople, once divided by routine, were united by the hilariously unpredictable turn their lives had taken.

Mayor Thompson, in a rare moment of reflection, looked out at the fairground from his office window. "Who would have thought that flying cows could bring us all together like this? Perhaps it's a reminder that life's most absurd moments can be the most magical."

Amidst the joy and laughter, a newcomer arrived in Mooington—a young woman named Lily, an aspiring artist with a heart full of dreams and an imagination to match. Lily had heard tales of the flying cows and had traveled from afar to witness the spectacle for herself.

With a sketchbook in hand, Lily wandered through the fairground, capturing the essence of Mooington's transformed spirit. She sketched children giggling as they rode the cow-themed rides and captured the camaraderie of townsfolk enjoying cow-shaped pastries.

As she sat by the pasture, sketching a contented cow that had taken a nap after a day of attention, Farmer Bob approached with a friendly smile. "Drawing our aerial bovines, I see?"

Lily nodded, her eyes sparkling with wonder. "There's something special about this place, about the cows... it's like they've shown us that dreams can truly take flight."

Farmer Bob chuckled. "Well, Lily, I reckon these cows have a way of reminding us that life's surprises are the ones worth celebrating."

As the sun dipped below the horizon, Lily shared her sketches with the townspeople, offering them a unique glimpse into the magic of Mooington. The sketches captured not just the cows, but the spirit of a community that had found joy in the unlikeliest of circumstances.

Chapter 4: The Curious Caper

As the days turned to weeks, Lily became an integral part of Mooington's vibrant tapestry. Her sketches, capturing the essence of the town and its flying cows, adorned the walls of local cafes and shops. She had a way of bringing out the quirky beauty of everyday moments, turning them into works of art that resonated with both locals and visitors.

One morning, Lily strolled through the town square, her sketchbook in hand, her eyes absorbing the colorful chaos around her. She noticed a group of children gathered in front of a makeshift stage, where a street performer was enthusiastically demonstrating juggling skills, using rubber chickens instead of balls.

Curiosity piqued, Lily joined the growing audience, chuckling along with the children's infectious laughter. She was so engrossed in the performance that she failed to notice a mischievous gust of wind carrying her sketchbook from her grasp.

The sketchbook soared into the air, performing an unintentional aerial dance of its own. Gasps filled the air as onlookers watched Lily's precious artwork perform a gravity-defying routine.

Across the square, a cow named Bessie, having recovered from her flying days, caught sight of the airborne sketchbook. With a determined look in her eyes, she sprang into action. With an expertly timed leap, Bessie managed to intercept the sketchbook mid-air, her wings flapping with unexpected finesse.

The crowd erupted into cheers and applause as Bessie landed gracefully, sketchbook held triumphantly in her mouth. Lily, a mixture of astonishment and gratitude on her face, approached the cow with a hearty laugh. "Well, I suppose even sketchbooks want to try their hand at flying in Mooington!"

The incident became the talk of the town, adding a new layer of amusement to the already bustling atmosphere. Lily immortalized the moment in a sketch, depicting Bessie's heroic mid-air rescue.

Meanwhile, Mayor Thompson had been busy coordinating Mooington's first-ever "Cow and Community" festival—a celebration that aimed to showcase not only the flying cows but also the unique camaraderie that had developed among the townspeople.

The festival preparations were in full swing, with stalls, games, and activities sprouting up throughout the town square. Lily found herself caught up in the excitement, helping to design banners and creating posters that depicted the cows as fearless aviators.

As the festival drew near, a sense of anticipation filled the air. Visitors from neighboring towns arrived, curious to experience the enchantment of Mooington firsthand. Local musicians tuned their instruments, and volunteers adorned themselves in cow-themed attire, ready to contribute to the whimsical festivities.

One evening, as the sun dipped below the horizon, Lily sat on a bench by the pasture, sketching a scene of cows frolicking beneath a sky ablaze with hues of pink and gold. Farmer Bob approached, a warm smile on his face.

"You've truly captured the heart of this place," he remarked, gazing at the sketch with a sense of pride. "And you've become a part of it too, Lily."

Lily looked up, a grateful smile curving her lips. "It's been a remarkable journey, Farmer Bob. Who would've thought that a town of flying cows could be so... magical?"

Farmer Bob chuckled. "Well, Lily, there's magic in the unexpected, and Mooington's got its fair share of that."

Chapter 5: Festival of Dreams

The sun rose on a day filled with excitement and anticipation in Mooington. The "Cow and Community" festival was in full swing, with the town square transformed into a kaleidoscope of colors, music, and laughter. Stalls offering cow-themed treats, games, and art displays lined the streets, while a stage stood ready for the evening's festivities.

Lily bustled about, helping set up a booth where festival-goers could try their hand at sketching their own flying cows. She marveled at the creativity of the townsfolk, who had transformed even the simplest of activities into uproarious games and imaginative challenges.

Mayor Thompson, wearing his most festive bowtie, stood at the festival's entrance, greeting visitors with enthusiasm. "Welcome, welcome, one and all, to our 'Cow and Community' festival! Prepare for a day of laughter, dreams, and a dash of the bovine!"

As the festival kicked off, Lily's sketching booth became a hit. Children and adults alike eagerly grabbed pencils, sketchpads, and their imaginations to create their own airborne bovines. The results ranged from hilariously abstract to surprisingly artistic, each sketch capturing the essence of Mooington's spirit.

Bessie the cow, now an unofficial festival mascot, wandered through the crowd with her wings held high, posing for photos and bringing smiles to all who encountered her. Even the pigeons seemed to have taken to her, occasionally perching on her back for a bird's-eye view of the festivities.

The highlight of the festival was a parade of flying cow floats, each creatively designed by the townspeople. From cow astronauts to cow superheroes, the floats showcased the unique charm of Mooington and its flying friends.

As the sun began to set, the stage came alive with music, and the townsfolk gathered for a talent show featuring cow-themed performances. The crowd erupted in applause as local musicians, singers, and even a few dancing cows took to the stage, delivering entertaining and often humorous acts.

Lily, too, found herself on stage, sharing her sketches with the audience. The sketches, displayed on a large screen, elicited laughter and appreciation, capturing the essence of the town's transformation in whimsical strokes of her pencil.

Amidst the festivities, Lily's eyes met those of a mysterious figure standing at the back of the crowd—an elderly man with a twinkle in his eye and a mischievous grin. He beckoned her over, and curiosity led Lily to his side.

"Enjoying the festival?" the man asked, his voice warm and friendly.

Lily nodded, still captivated by the energy and joy surrounding her. "It's been incredible, more than I could have imagined."

The man chuckled. "Ah, young lady, this town has a way of turning even the most ordinary of things into something extraordinary."

As the evening's celebrations continued, Lily couldn't shake the feeling that there was more to this enigmatic stranger than met the eye. But the festival was in full swing, and she was caught up in the joyous spirit of the moment.

Chapter 6: Whispers of Wonder

The festival had come to an end, leaving Mooington bathed in the glow of the setting sun. As the last notes of music faded into the evening air, the townsfolk exchanged smiles, their hearts full of shared memories and newfound connections.

Lily walked through the now-quiet town square, the remnants of the festival scattered around her like fragments of a dream. She couldn't help but feel a sense of contentment and gratitude for the time she had spent in Mooington, capturing its essence with her sketches.

As she passed by the pasture, she noticed the mysterious man she had encountered during the festival. He stood by the fence, his gaze fixed on the horizon as if lost in thought. Intrigued, Lily approached him.

"Quite a festival, wasn't it?" she ventured, a warm smile on her lips.

The man turned to her, his eyes twinkling with a mixture of wisdom and whimsy. "Indeed, a festival that has woven even more threads into the tapestry of Mooington."

Lily's curiosity piqued. "You seem to know a lot about this town."

The man chuckled softly. "I've known this town longer than most. You could say I've been a silent observer of its transformations."

Lily's eyebrows arched. "Are you a historian or perhaps a wandering philosopher?"

The man's grin widened. "You might say I'm a collector of stories—stories that hold the essence of places and people."

Lily's intuition tingled. "And what stories does Mooington hold for you?"

The man's gaze turned distant, his voice carrying a hint of nostalgia. "Mooington is a place where the ordinary becomes extraordinary. Where dreams take flight, not just for cows, but for all who find themselves entwined in its whimsy."

Lily's heart skipped a beat. "You make it sound like you're not just an observer, but a part of the story."

The man's eyes twinkled knowingly. "Perhaps I am, in a way."

Before Lily could inquire further, the man's attention shifted to the sky. "Look up, Lily. Do you see it?"

Lily followed his gaze, her eyes widening as she noticed a formation of clouds—clouds that seemed to resemble the shape of a cow with outstretched wings. It was as if the sky itself was painting a portrait of Mooington's whimsical inhabitants.

"It's... it's incredible," Lily whispered, her heart brimming with wonder.

The man nodded. "Sometimes, stories linger not just in words, but in the very fabric of the world around us."

As the sun dipped below the horizon, casting a warm glow over Mooington, the man turned to Lily with a gentle smile. "Lily, remember that every place has its own magic—a magic that lingers in the moments shared, the dreams pursued, and the laughter echoed."

Lily's gaze remained fixed on the sky, the vision of the cloud-formed cow etched into her memory. She knew that her time in Mooington had left an indelible mark on her heart, and the mysteries woven into the town's whimsical charm would remain with her forever.

Chapter 7: Echoes of the Heart

The days in Mooington settled into a gentle rhythm, much like the comforting mooing of contented cows in a serene pasture. Lily continued to sketch and connect with the townsfolk, the memories of the festival and the mysterious man lingering in her thoughts.

One afternoon, as Lily sat by the pasture, sketching a scene of cows basking in the afternoon sun, Farmer Bob approached with a knowing smile. "Lily, there's something I'd like to show you."

Curiosity piqued, Lily followed Farmer Bob to a quiet corner of the pasture. There, beneath the shade of a sprawling oak tree, lay a collection of weathered journals. The pages were filled with handwritten stories, sketches, and snippets of wisdom.

"These journals have been passed down through generations," Farmer Bob explained. "They hold the tales of Mooington—the dreams, the laughter, and the moments that have shaped this town."

Lily's eyes widened in awe as she flipped through the pages. Each entry was a glimpse into the lives of Mooington's inhabitants, capturing their joys, their quirks, and the enduring spirit of the town.

"These journals are a part of Mooington's legacy," Farmer Bob continued. "And it's time for you to add your chapter to this tapestry of stories."

Lily blinked, surprised. "Me? But I'm just a visitor."

Farmer Bob chuckled. "Sometimes, it takes an outsider's perspective to see the magic that's been here all along. Your sketches, your observations—they're a testament to the way you've embraced Mooington's spirit."

As Lily leafed through the journals, she realized that each entry was a whisper of the heart, a testament to the connections formed, the dreams pursued, and the joy shared. She knew that she had been woven into the fabric of Mooington's story, just as the town had become a part of hers.

That night, Lily found herself beneath the starlit sky, surrounded by the gentle rustling of leaves and the distant murmur of cows. She held her own journal in her hands, the blank pages awaiting her thoughts and sketches.

With a sense of purpose, Lily began to write—a letter to Mooington, a tribute to the friendships forged, the laughter echoed, and the lessons learned. She poured her heart onto the pages, her words a reflection of the magic she had found in this whimsical town.

As the ink flowed, Lily felt a connection that transcended words—a connection to Mooington's past, present, and future. She knew that her story, like those of the townsfolk before her, would become a part of Mooington's legacy, whispered through the generations.

Chapter 8: The Legacy Takes Flight

As days turned into weeks, Lily continued to immerse herself in the life of Mooington. Her sketches adorned the town's walls, capturing the charm of its flying cows, its bustling streets, and its heartwarming moments. The legacy of the festival lived on in the hearts of the townsfolk, and Lily's own journal entries had become a part of Mooington's treasured collection.

One evening, Lily found herself in the town square, gazing up at the stars that twinkled like distant fireflies. The air was filled with a sense of nostalgia, a bittersweet feeling that often accompanies the end of a journey.

Bessie, the cow who had become a symbol of Mooington's whimsy, approached Lily with a nudge and a friendly moo. Lily chuckled, her fingers absently stroking the cow's soft fur. "You're quite the star, aren't you?"

As if in response, a shooting star streaked across the sky, leaving a trail of brilliance in its wake. Lily closed her eyes, making a silent wish that the enchantment of Mooington would endure, that its spirit of camaraderie and laughter would continue to shape the town's future.

In the distance, the mysterious man she had encountered during the festival stood beneath the lamplight, his presence a comforting presence in the tranquil night. He walked over to Lily, his gaze fixed on the stars.

"Mooington has a way of leaving a mark, doesn't it?" he mused.

Lily nodded, her heart filled with a mixture of gratitude and wistfulness. "It's a place that reminds us to find joy in the unexpected and to cherish the connections we make."

The man smiled, his eyes reflecting the wisdom of ages. "Sometimes, all it takes is a touch of whimsy to bring out the beauty that's already there."

As they stood side by side, gazing at the night sky, a soft melody carried by the wind reached their ears. The townspeople had gathered for an impromptu musical gathering, their voices harmonizing in a song that echoed through the streets—a song of unity, of dreams, and of the bonds that tied them together.

Lily turned to the man, a question in her eyes. "Who are you, really? Why are you so connected to Mooington?"

The man's smile held a touch of mystery. "Perhaps I'm a reflection of the town's spirit, a wanderer who finds solace in its laughter and its dreams."

Lily nodded, feeling a sense of closure and acceptance. She knew that some mysteries were meant to remain unsolved, to be embraced as part of the enchantment of life itself.

As the night deepened, Lily and the man walked through the quiet streets of Mooington, their footsteps accompanied by the gentle mooing of cows. The legacy of the festival, the whispers of the journals, and the echoes of laughter seemed to envelop them, creating a sense of timeless connection.

Chapter 8: Whispers of Forever

As the days grew longer in Mooington, a gentle breeze carried with it a sense of change. The town was bathed in the hues of summer, its streets bustling with the laughter of children and the hum of excitement. Among the townsfolk, a new sentiment seemed to be stirring—the kindling of a different kind of magic.

Lily found herself drawn to the town's gazebo one evening, its white latticework bathed in the soft glow of twilight. She sat on a bench, her sketchbook resting on her lap, lost in thought. The enchantment of Mooington had seeped into her heart, its memories a tapestry she cherished.

Footsteps approached, and Lily looked up to find the mysterious man standing before her, a small bouquet of wildflowers in his hands. "I thought you might like these," he said, offering her the flowers with a warm smile.

Lily accepted them, her heart skipping a beat at his thoughtful gesture. "Thank you. They're beautiful."

The man took a seat beside her, his gaze fixed on the horizon. "Lily, there's something I haven't told you."

Lily turned to him, curiosity in her eyes. "What is it?"

He hesitated, as if choosing his words carefully. "I've spent many lifetimes wandering through different places, collecting stories and moments. But it's here in Mooington that I've felt a connection that goes beyond the ordinary."

Lily's heart raced, sensing that his words held a deeper meaning. "What kind of connection?"

The man looked at her, his gaze gentle and sincere. "A connection that's not bound by time or logic—a connection that feels like... destiny."

Lily's breath caught, her heart pounding in her chest. "Destiny?"

He nodded, his expression earnest. "Yes, destiny. Lily, the magic of Mooington isn't just in its flying cows or its festivals. It's in the way it brings people together, in the way it ignites dreams and kindles friendships."

Lily's mind raced, her heart torn between the enchantment of the town and the pull of the man's presence. She remembered the shooting star and the wishes she had made. Could it be that the unexpected magic of Mooington had a role in weaving their paths together?

The man reached out, his hand gently touching hers, sending a shiver of warmth through her. "Lily, I believe that some connections are written in the stars, meant to unfold in ways we can't fully comprehend."

Their eyes locked, and in that moment, the world seemed to stand still. The breeze carried with it the whispers of dreams and the echoes of laughter, intertwining with the beating of their hearts.

As the night deepened, they sat there, lost in each other's company, their conversation a dance of shared thoughts and unspoken emotions. The stars above seemed to shimmer with a knowing twinkle, as if they too were witnesses to the magic of that moment.

Chapter 9: Of Laughter and Love

The days in Mooington continued to unfold like a charming tale, each moment woven with the threads of whimsy and wonder. Lily and the mysterious man found themselves spending more time together, exploring the town's nooks and crannies, and discovering the hidden corners where laughter seemed to linger.

One sunny afternoon, Lily and the man embarked on a leisurely stroll through the meadows surrounding Mooington. The wildflowers swayed in the breeze, and the soft mooing of distant cows created a soothing backdrop.

As they walked, Lily couldn't help but notice a makeshift seesaw nestled among the grass. It was a simple contraption, formed from a wooden plank and a large log, clearly crafted by the town's inventive minds.

Lily's eyes twinkled with mischief as she turned to the man. "Would you like to have a go on the seesaw?"

The man raised an eyebrow, his expression a mix of surprise and amusement. "A seesaw? You're suggesting we partake in some childhood merriment?"

Lily nodded, her laughter contagious. "Why not? After all, Mooington's magic is all about embracing the unexpected."

The man chuckled, his eyes crinkling with laughter. "Very well, let's give it a try."

With a shared sense of spontaneity, Lily and the man positioned themselves on opposite ends of the seesaw. The plank creaked beneath them as they shifted their weight, causing the log on the other side to rise. Balancing precariously, they exchanged amused glances before breaking into laughter.

Up and down they went, their laughter rising and falling in harmony with the seesaw's motion. With each movement, they seemed to shed the weight of adulthood, embracing the carefree joy of the moment.

Suddenly, a loud "Moo!" interrupted their mirth. Bessie had sauntered over, her wings flapping as she observed the comical scene. She seemed to tilt her head in bemusement, as if wondering why humans found such amusement in a simple seesaw.

Lily and the man couldn't contain their laughter, the sight of Bessie's bewildered expression only adding to the comedy. They continued their seesaw escapade, the laughter echoing through the meadow, carrying with it the magic of shared moments.

As the sun began to dip below the horizon, casting a warm golden glow, Lily and the man found themselves sitting on the grass, their laughter gradually subsiding into contented smiles.

"You know," Lily began, her eyes twinkling, "I think we've officially become part of Mooington's charming oddities."

The man chuckled, his gaze fixed on the sky. "And why not? After all, it's the oddities that make life truly enchanting."

Lily nodded in agreement, her heart swelling with affection for the man and the town that had become her unexpected haven. She realized that in the midst of laughter, shared silliness, and moments of pure whimsy, something beautiful was blossoming between them—a connection that defied explanation and radiated with warmth.

Chapter 10: Whispers of Serendipity

The days in Mooington carried with them a sense of enchantment that seemed to deepen with each passing moment. Lily and the mysterious man found themselves falling into a rhythm of shared laughter, stolen glances, and conversations that flowed effortlessly.

One evening, as the sun painted the sky in shades of orange and pink, Lily and the man sat on a hill overlooking the town. The air was filled with the mingling scents of wildflowers and fresh grass, and the town square below buzzed with activity as the townsfolk went about their evening routines.

Lily turned to the man, a contemplative look in her eyes. "You know, I've spent a lot of time sketching the town and its people, but I've never actually tried flying with the cows."

The man chuckled softly. "Flying with cows? That does sound like an adventure."

Lily grinned, her eyes alight with mischief. "Well, they say that embracing Mooington's whimsy can lead to unexpected discoveries."

The man raised an eyebrow, his curiosity piqued. "Are you suggesting that we... fly with the cows?"

Lily's laughter danced on the wind. "Why not? It's the perfect way to experience Mooington's magic up close."

Before the man could respond, a soft rustling of wings caught their attention. Bessie the cow, her wings spread wide, approached them with an inquisitive moo. It was as if she had heard their conversation and was eager to join in the fun.

Lily and the man exchanged amused glances before looking back at Bessie. "What do you say, Bessie?" Lily asked, her voice laced with excitement.

Bessie mooed in response, flapping her wings as if to signal her approval. Lily's heart raced, a sense of exhilaration coursing through her veins.

With a shared sense of spontaneity, Lily and the man climbed onto Bessie's back, gripping her feathers for balance. The wind ruffled their hair as Bessie's wings beat in a steady rhythm, carrying them into the air.

The sensation was unlike anything Lily had ever experienced. The world below seemed to shrink as they soared higher, the town of Mooington a whimsical tapestry of color and life. Laughter bubbled from their lips, carried away by the wind, as they marveled at the town's beauty from a new perspective.

As they glided through the sky, Lily turned to the man, her eyes sparkling with joy. "This is incredible! It's like living out a dream."

The man's smile was a reflection of her own delight. "Mooington has a way of turning dreams into reality."

Their flight with Bessie was a symphony of laughter and wonder, a testament to the boundless magic of the town they had both come to love. And as they gently landed back on the hill, breathless and exhilarated, Lily and the man shared a moment that seemed to encapsulate the essence of their connection—an unspoken understanding that transcended words.

As the sun dipped below the horizon, casting a warm glow over Mooington, Lily and the man stood side by side, their hearts aligned with the rhythm of the town. They knew that their journey was far from over, that the magic of Mooington had become a part of their story in ways they couldn't fully comprehend.

Chapter 11: Echoes of Destiny

The revelation hung in the air like a storm cloud, casting a shadow over the enchantment that had surrounded Mooington. Lily's heart raced as she looked at the man before her, his eyes holding a mixture of sadness and resignation.

"What do you mean your time here is limited?" Lily's voice trembled with a mix of emotions—confusion, fear, and a deep sense of concern.

The man sighed, his gaze fixed on the horizon as if grappling with his own thoughts. "Mooington's magic and my presence are intertwined, but it's not a permanent bond. I exist here for a purpose, and once that purpose is fulfilled, I'll have to leave."

Lily's mind raced, her thoughts a whirlwind of questions. "But why? Why would you have to leave? And what's this purpose you're talking about?"

The man's lips formed a somber smile. "It's a complicated tale, Lily. One that spans generations and is woven into the very fabric of this town. My presence here is connected to Mooington's history, its magic, and the destiny that has been set in motion long before my time."

Lily's heart ached at the weight of his words. The town that had come to mean so much to her was entangled in a web of secrets, and the man she had grown to care for was a part of its enigmatic narrative.

"Why didn't you tell me this before?" Lily's voice quivered, a mix of hurt and frustration evident in her tone.

The man turned to her, his gaze earnest. "I wanted to shield you from the complexities, to give you a chance to experience the beauty of Mooington without the burden of its secrets. But I realize now that keeping the truth from you was a mistake."

Lily's emotions were a whirlpool of conflicting feelings—anger at being kept in the dark, sadness for the man's plight, and a deep longing for the connection they had forged.

"Is there any way to change your fate?" Lily's voice was a whisper, her eyes searching his for a glimmer of hope.

The man's expression softened, his fingers gently brushing against hers. "I don't know, Lily. The tapestry of destiny is intricate and unforgiving. All I can do is fulfill my purpose here and hope that it leads to a resolution."

Lily's heart ached as she looked at the man, the weight of their shared moments and unspoken emotions hanging heavily between them. The enchantment of Mooington seemed to have taken on a bittersweet quality, its magic tinged with the reality of their circumstances.

As the sun dipped below the horizon, casting long shadows over Mooington, Lily and the man found themselves sitting in the quiet embrace of the hill. The echoes of their conversation lingered in the air, a reminder of the fragility of their connection and the secrets that bound them.

Chapter 12: Torn Threads

Days turned into nights, and the weight of the revelation hung heavily over Mooington. Lily found herself torn between the enchantment that had drawn her to the town and the reality of the man's limited presence. Every smile they shared, every stolen glance, felt like a fragile thread that could be unravelled at any moment.

Lily had spent hours pouring over her sketches, the memories of their time together etched onto paper. She wandered through the town's streets, each corner a reminder of the laughter they had shared and the moments they had treasured. And yet, the shadow of the man's impending departure loomed large, casting a pall over the whimsy that had once felt so pure.

One evening, as the sun began its descent, Lily found herself on the hill where they had once flown with Bessie. She stared out at the town, the gentle breeze carrying with it a sense of melancholy.

The man appeared beside her, his expression a mixture of sadness and determination. "Lily, I need to talk to you."

Lily turned to him, her heart aching at the sight of his troubled gaze. "What is it?"

He took a deep breath, his eyes searching hers. "My time in Mooington is drawing to a close, and with it, the bond that has connected us."

Tears welled in Lily's eyes, her voice cracking as she spoke. "Is there really no way to change your fate? No way for you to stay?"

The man's gaze was filled with regret. "The tapestry of destiny is intricate, Lily. Changing its course would require a sacrifice—one that I can't ask you to make."

Lily's heart clenched at his words, the weight of the choice before her like an anchor. She had come to love Mooington and the man who had become a part of its magic, and now she faced a decision that could alter the course of their intertwined destinies.

As they stood there, the sky painted in hues of orange and gold, the world seemed to hold its breath—a quiet moment suspended in time. Lily's mind was a whirlwind of emotions, a storm of longing and heartache.

The man's fingers brushed against hers, his touch gentle and comforting. "I wish things were different, Lily. I wish I could stay and see where our connection leads."

Lily's voice was a whisper, a fragile thread of emotion. "And I wish I could make the choice that would allow you to stay."

They stood there, the weight of unspoken words and unfulfilled wishes hanging heavily between them. The sun dipped below the horizon, casting a shroud of darkness over Mooington.

Chapter 13: Unraveled Desires

The air in Mooington seemed heavy with anticipation, every corner of the town tinged with the bittersweet knowledge that change was on the horizon. Lily's heart felt like a pendulum, swinging between the enchantment of the place she had come to call home and the reality of the man's impending departure.

As the days passed, Lily found herself seeking solace in the places that held memories of their time together. She wandered through the town square, where the laughter of children and the melodies of street musicians mingled in the air. Yet, the echoes of their laughter and shared conversations seemed distant now, a reminder of the impending loss that hovered over them.

One evening, Lily sat on a bench by the fountain, her gaze fixed on the water's shimmering surface. She felt a presence beside her and turned to find the man, his expression a blend of longing and resignation.

"Lily," he began, his voice a mixture of sorrow and affection, "I wish there was a way to change what's inevitable."

Lily's heart clenched as she looked at him, her voice filled with emotion. "I can't bear the thought of you leaving, of our connection fading away."

The man's fingers brushed against hers, the touch sending a shiver down her spine. "I know how much Mooington has come to mean to you, and I want you to remember the magic—the laughter, the joy—without the weight of my departure tainting it."

Tears welled in Lily's eyes, a mixture of sorrow and frustration. "How can I forget you? How can I forget the way you've become a part of this place, a part of my heart?"

The man's gaze was intense, his eyes locked on hers. "Lily, you are the most unexpected and beautiful part of my time in Mooington. I wish I could stay, but sometimes destiny is a force too strong to defy."

Lily's fingers tightened around his, their connection a lifeline in the storm of emotions. "Is there nothing we can do? No way to change your fate?"

The man's expression held a hint of a sad smile. "Perhaps the threads of destiny are not unyielding. But to alter them would require a sacrifice—one that I can't ask you to make."

Lily's mind was a whirlwind of thoughts, her heart torn between her love for Mooington and her growing attachment to the man who had become its enigmatic part. She closed her eyes, feeling the weight of her choices pressing down on her.

As they sat there, the moon casting a gentle glow over the town, Lily and the man found themselves at the intersection of love and fate, their hearts entwined in a complex dance. The enchantment of Mooington seemed to hold its breath, waiting for the path to unfold.

Chapter 13: Unraveled Desires

The air in Mooington seemed heavy with anticipation, every corner of the town tinged with the bittersweet knowledge that change was on the horizon. Lily's heart felt like a pendulum, swinging between the enchantment of the place she had come to call home and the reality of the man's impending departure.

As the days passed, Lily found herself seeking solace in the places that held memories of their time together. She wandered through the town square, where the laughter of children and the melodies of street musicians mingled in the air. Yet, the echoes of their laughter and shared conversations seemed distant now, a reminder of the impending loss that hovered over them.

One evening, Lily sat on a bench by the fountain, her gaze fixed on the water's shimmering surface. She felt a presence beside her and turned to find the man, his expression a blend of longing and resignation.

"Gabriel," she whispered his name, her voice tinged with both sorrow and affection.

Gabriel's fingers brushed against hers, the touch sending a shiver down her spine. "Lily, I wish there was a way to change what's inevitable."

Lily's heart clenched as she looked at him, her voice filled with emotion. "I can't bear the thought of you leaving, of our connection fading away."

Gabriel's gaze was intense, his eyes locked on hers. "I know how much Mooington has come to mean to you, and I want you to remember the magic—the laughter, the joy—without the weight of my departure tainting it."

Tears welled in Lily's eyes, a mixture of sorrow and frustration. "How can I forget you? How can I forget the way you've become a part of this place, a part of my heart?"

Gabriel's fingers tightened around hers, their connection a lifeline in the storm of emotions. "Lily, you are the most unexpected and beautiful part of my time in Mooington. I wish I could stay, but sometimes destiny is a force too strong to defy."

Lily's mind was a whirlwind of thoughts, her heart torn between her love for Mooington and her growing attachment to Gabriel, the man who had become its enigmatic part. She closed her eyes, feeling the weight of her choices pressing down on her.

As they sat there, the moon casting a gentle glow over the town, Lily and Gabriel found themselves at the intersection of love and fate, their hearts entwined in a complex dance. The enchantment of Mooington seemed to hold its breath, waiting for the path to unfold.

Chapter 14: Echoes of Departure

The days in Mooington grew quieter, the enchantment that had once filled the air now tinged with a sense of melancholy. Lily walked through the streets, her heart heavy with the absence of the man who had become an integral part of the town's magic.

The townsfolk noticed the change in Lily, the way her laughter seemed to have lost its sparkle and her sketches held a touch of sadness. Bessie, the flying cow, would occasionally flap her wings and nuzzle Lily as if to offer comfort in her own unique way.

One evening, Lily stood on the hill overlooking Mooington, the memories of her time with Gabriel a bittersweet ache in her heart. The sun painted the sky in shades of pink and gold, casting a warm glow over the town.

As she gazed at the sunset, a familiar figure appeared by her side. It was Isaac, the local storyteller, his eyes kind and understanding.

"Lily," he began, his voice gentle, "I've noticed the change in you. Mooington has a way of weaving connections that run deep."

Lily offered him a small smile, her eyes holding a mix of gratitude and sorrow. "Gabriel was a part of that connection. He brought something magical to this place."

Isaac nodded, his gaze fixed on the horizon. "Every story has its moments of joy and sorrow. The threads of fate can be complex, and sometimes they lead us to unexpected places."

Lily's voice was a whisper, her thoughts a tumultuous storm. "I miss him. I miss the laughter and the way he made me see Mooington in a different light."

Isaac's expression was one of understanding. "Gabriel's presence may have faded, but the magic he brought to Mooington lives on. And who's to say what the future holds? Perhaps destiny has more in store for you."

Lily looked at Isaac, her heart both heavy and hopeful. The town that had become her refuge was a tapestry of memories, a canvas onto which she had painted moments of laughter, wonder, and love.

As the sun set, casting a gentle farewell to the day, Lily knew that Mooington's enchantment had changed her in ways she could never have anticipated. The town held a piece of her heart, and the echoes of Gabriel's presence were woven into its very fabric.

Chapter 15: Serendipitous Laughter

Mooington's streets were no longer filled with just sorrow; a subtle shift had occurred. Lily found herself drawn to the town's quirkiness, its inherent ability to weave moments of humor into the fabric of everyday life. The townsfolk seemed to have taken it upon themselves to lift Lily's spirits, and laughter began to fill the air once more.

One morning, Lily wandered into the town square, her steps lighter than they had been in days. As she passed the bakery, a mischievous grin tugged at the corner of her lips. A crowd had gathered around a vendor who was showcasing an assortment of baked goods, each one adorned with whimsical designs.

"Behold, the flying cow croissants!" the vendor declared, holding up pastries shaped like cows with wings.

The townspeople erupted in laughter, and Lily couldn't help but join in. The sight of the comical croissants and the infectious joy of the crowd was like a balm to her soul.

Isaac, the storyteller, appeared at her side, his eyes twinkling with mischief. "I see the town's whimsy is working its magic on you."

Lily chuckled, the weight that had been pressing on her heart beginning to lift. "It's hard not to smile when Mooington is determined to make you laugh."

Isaac nodded, his gaze sweeping over the crowd. "Laughter is the heart's way of healing, and this town has a knack for turning even the simplest moments into something special."

As Lily watched the townspeople indulge in the flying cow croissants, she couldn't help but appreciate the way Mooington embraced life's quirks with open arms. The bakery vendor continued to entertain the crowd, his jokes and playful banter creating an atmosphere of joy.

Later that day, as Lily sat in the town square sketching the scene, Bessie, the flying cow, appeared beside her with a mischievous moo. Lily laughed, reaching out to pet her feathery wings. "Are you here to remind me that life's adventures can be both unexpected and funny?"

Bessie mooed as if in agreement, flapping her wings in a playful dance.

Lily continued to sketch, her heart feeling lighter than it had in weeks. The comedy of the flying cow croissants was a reminder that even in moments of loss, there was room for laughter and joy.

Chapter 17: The Great Mooington Mischief

The air in Mooington was filled with a palpable sense of anticipation. The townsfolk had been whispering and giggling, their eyes glinting with mischief. Lily couldn't help but feel a sense of curiosity as she wandered through the streets, wondering what could be causing such excitement.

As she passed by the town's central square, Lily's eyes widened at the sight before her. A makeshift stage had been set up, and a banner overhead read: "The Great Mooington Mischief Show."

Isaac, the local storyteller, stood at the center of the stage, his posture exuding a blend of seriousness and theatrics. The townspeople had gathered around, their expressions a mix of anticipation and glee.

"Welcome, dear friends, to a display of Mooington's finest and most hilarious antics!" Isaac declared, his voice carrying a theatrical flourish.

Lily couldn't suppress a chuckle as she joined the growing crowd. Whatever this "mischief show" was, it promised to be a delightful diversion.

Isaac's storytelling prowess was on full display as he recounted tales of comical mishaps and hilarious misunderstandings that had occurred in Mooington over the years. The townspeople roared with laughter, their spirits lifted by the infectious energy of the performance.

Lily watched with amusement as Isaac pantomimed various scenarios, his exaggerated expressions causing fits of laughter among the audience. The stories ranged from cows mysteriously appearing on rooftops to mishaps with enchanted brooms that had a mind of their own.

As the show reached its peak, Isaac announced a grand finale that had the crowd buzzing with excitement. "And now, for the pièce de résistance—a reenactment of the day when a group of townsfolk accidentally painted the town square pink instead of blue!"

Lily's eyes widened as a group of villagers stepped onto the stage, wearing elaborate costumes and wielding paintbrushes. The townsfolk in the audience erupted into laughter, recalling the infamous incident that had become a legendary tale in Mooington.

The reenactment was a riot of exaggerated movements, colorful props, and uproarious laughter. Lily found herself laughing along with the crowd, the carefree spirit of the event infectious.

As the performance came to an end, Isaac took a bow amid cheers and applause. Lily approached him with a grin, unable to contain her amusement. "Isaac, that was absolutely brilliant! I haven't laughed like that in a long time."

Isaac returned her smile, his eyes twinkling with mischief. "Laughter is a gift, my dear. And Mooington has a way of reminding us to embrace life's lighter moments."

As the sun began to set, casting a warm glow over the town, Lily felt a renewed sense of appreciation for Mooington's whimsy. The "Great Mooington Mischief Show" had turned the ordinary into the extraordinary, reminding her that even in the face of challenges, laughter and lightheartedness had the power to heal.

Chapter 18: The Whimsical Quest

Mooington's streets were abuzz with a new sense of excitement. A colorful array of posters had been plastered around town, each one adorned with vibrant illustrations and whimsical fonts. The message was clear: "Join the Whimsical Quest for the Elusive Dancing Cheese!"

Lily's curiosity was piqued as she studied the posters, her lips curling into a smile. It seemed that Mooington was about to embark on another one of its lighthearted escapades.

As she made her way to the town square, Lily found the townspeople gathered, each one dressed in an array of imaginative costumes. Isaac, the local storyteller, stood at the center, wearing a cape adorned with sparkles and a hat that defied gravity.

"Ladies and gentlemen, boys and girls, and creatures of all whimsy!" Isaac's voice rang out, his theatrics taking center stage once again. "Today, we embark on a quest like no other—a quest for the elusive dancing cheese!"

Lily couldn't help but chuckle at the absurdity of the concept. A quest for a dancing cheese? Only in Mooington could such an idea take root.

Isaac continued to explain the rules of the quest—participants would follow a series of whimsical clues that would lead them on a journey through the town's nooks and crannies. The prize? The honor of discovering the legendary dancing cheese.

Lily decided to join in the fun, donning a costume that was a mix of a pirate and a fairy, complete with a hat adorned with feathers and a toy sword at her side.

As the quest kicked off, Lily found herself giggling at the sight of townsfolk searching for clues with a blend of determination and hilarity. Each clue was a riddle that led them to different corners of Mooington, from the bakery to the town library.

At one point, Lily found herself in a whimsical tea party hosted by a group of elderly ladies who insisted on sharing stories of their own quests for dancing cheeses in their youth. The tales were a mix of absurdity and heartwarming nostalgia, and Lily couldn't help but marvel at the way Mooington's magic had a way of turning the ordinary into the extraordinary.

As the quest continued, Lily's heart felt lighter than it had in weeks. The camaraderie among the townspeople, the laughter that echoed through the streets—it was a reminder that even in the face of challenges, Mooington's whimsy could bring people together in unexpected ways.

Finally, after a series of clues that led participants through a hilarious series of misadventures, the quest culminated in the town square. Isaac stood at the center, holding a tray with a plate of cheese that seemed to be swaying in time with a playful melody.

"Ladies and gentlemen, creatures of whimsy, behold—the Dancing Cheese!" Isaac announced, his voice a mix of amusement and theatrical flair.

The townsfolk erupted into laughter and applause, their joy infectious. Lily couldn't help but join in, her heart warmed by the collective spirit of silliness that had taken over Mooington.

Chapter 19: The Giggle Gala

Mooington's enchantment continued to weave its whimsy into the fabric of everyday life. The town square was once again transformed, this time into a vibrant spectacle of colorful decorations, twinkling lights, and a stage adorned with playful banners. The posters around town bore the announcement: "Get ready for the Giggle Gala!"

Lily couldn't help but smile as she read the words. It seemed that Mooington had decided to throw another one of its uproarious celebrations, and she was eager to be a part of it.

As she approached the town square, Lily was met with a sight that left her grinning from ear to ear. The townsfolk had gone all out with their costumes, each one more outrageous and hilarious than the last. There were clowns, animals in tutus, and even a group dressed as oversized vegetables.

Isaac, the master of ceremonies, stood on the stage wearing a rainbow-colored suit and a top hat that defied gravity. He twirled his mustache and greeted the crowd with a flourish.

"Ladies and gentlemen, whimsical beings, and lovers of laughter, welcome to the Giggle Gala!" Isaac's voice boomed, his enthusiasm contagious.

Lily found herself swept up in the energy of the event, joining the crowd in cheers and laughter. The air was filled with a sense of anticipation, a promise of an evening filled with merriment and mirth.

The Gala kicked off with a series of slapstick comedy acts that had the audience doubled over with laughter. Juggling clowns, pratfalls, and a synchronized dance routine that defied all logic—the performances were a riotous blend of absurdity and skill.

Lily watched with glee as townsfolk and visitors alike joined in the fun. There was a pie-eating contest that resulted in whipped cream-covered faces, a balloon animal-making competition that led to the creation of some truly bizarre creatures, and a tug-of-war that became a comical battle of wits.

As the evening progressed, Isaac announced a surprise event that had everyone buzzing with excitement. "Ladies and gentlemen, prepare yourselves for the ultimate test of laughter—the Giggle-Off!"

Participants were invited to take the stage one by one, armed with their best jokes and puns. The audience erupted into laughter with each punchline, and Lily found herself clutching her sides as tears of mirth streamed down her face.

When it was her turn, Lily stepped onto the stage, her heart pounding with a mix of nerves and excitement. She cleared her throat and delivered a classic knock-knock joke that had been her childhood favorite. The audience roared with laughter, and Lily couldn't help but laugh along with them.

As the night wore on, the laughter seemed to mingle with the stars, creating an atmosphere of pure joy and camaraderie. The Giggle Gala was a testament to the town's ability to create moments of merriment out of thin air, to turn the ordinary into the extraordinary with a dash of humor.

Chapter 20: The Chuckle Chronicles

Mooington's streets were still echoing with the lingering laughter from the Giggle Gala. The town's enchantment had taken on a new dimension—one of joy, camaraderie, and an unyielding dedication to finding humor in every corner of life.

Lily found herself walking through the town square, her steps light and her heart full of the memories of the uproarious evening. As she passed the bookstore, a new display caught her eye. A colorful sign read: "The Chuckle Chronicles—a collection of Mooington's funniest stories!"

Intrigued, Lily stepped into the bookstore, her eyes scanning the shelves for the promised collection. A friendly bookseller approached her, a mischievous twinkle in her eyes.

"Ah, you're looking for the Chuckle Chronicles, I see!" the bookseller exclaimed. "A delightful selection of anecdotes and tales that capture the essence of Mooington's humor."

Lily nodded with a smile, her curiosity piqued. She had a feeling that the stories within the Chronicles would be just as whimsical and amusing as the town itself.

As she settled into a cozy reading nook, Lily opened the book to the first page and began to read. The tales ranged from hilarious mishaps during the annual Mooington Pie Baking Contest to the comical encounters between townspeople and the town's ever-playful squirrels.

Each story was a testament to the town's ability to find laughter in the most unexpected places. Lily found herself chuckling at the descriptions of quirky characters and the outrageous situations they found themselves in. The Chuckle Chronicles seemed to capture the very essence of Mooington's spirit—a celebration of the absurd and a reminder that life's challenges could be met with a dose of humor.

As she continued to read, Lily's laughter mingled with the gentle rustling of pages and the distant sounds of Mooington's bustling streets. The Chuckle Chronicles had a way of lifting her spirits and reminding her that even in moments of uncertainty, there was room for joy and lightheartedness.

After hours spent lost in the world of Mooington's funniest stories, Lily closed the book with a contented sigh. She felt a renewed appreciation for the town's enchantment, for the way it had embraced the power of laughter to bring people together.

As she stepped back into the sunlight, Lily couldn't help but smile at the thought of the Chuckle Chronicles finding their way into the hands of townsfolk and visitors alike. The stories were a reminder that even in the midst of life's complexities, Mooington's magic could always be counted on to deliver a good laugh.

Chapter 21: The Whimsical Race

The sun shone brightly over Mooington, casting a warm glow on the town's bustling streets. The enchantment of the place had taken on a new twist, one that involved a combination of laughter, camaraderie, and a touch of friendly competition.

Lily found herself drawn to the town square once again, where a lively crowd had gathered. The posters around town had announced the day's event: "The Whimsical Race—a challenge of laughter, agility, and all-around absurdity!"

As she joined the crowd, Lily couldn't help but chuckle at the sight of the makeshift racecourse that had been set up. It was a maze of obstacles that ranged from giant inflatable cushions to wobbly bridges made of pool noodles.

Isaac, the town's beloved storyteller, stood at the center of the chaos, his colorful outfit making him look like a cross between a ringmaster and a mad scientist.

"Ladies and gentlemen, beings of whimsy, and seekers of the absurd, welcome to the Whimsical Race!" Isaac declared, his voice a mixture of enthusiasm and theatrical flair.

Lily grinned as she listened to Isaac explain the rules of the race. Teams of townsfolk and visitors were to navigate the racecourse, completing challenges that were designed to elicit laughter and showcase their agility. The goal was not just to win, but to enjoy every hilarious moment along the way.

Lily decided to join a team and found herself donning a ridiculous costume that involved a tutu, a cape, and a pair of oversized sunglasses. As the race began, she couldn't suppress her laughter at the sight of her fellow competitors dressed in equally outrageous attire.

The challenges were a blend of physical feats and comedic mishaps. Teams had to balance on a seesaw while reciting silly rhymes, navigate a maze of giant rubber ducks, and even attempt a three-legged race while holding a balloon between their heads.

Lily's team found themselves in fits of laughter as they stumbled through the obstacles, their determination mixed with hilarity. The race was a whirlwind of absurdity, a testament to Mooington's ability to infuse even the most competitive events with a sense of lightheartedness.

As the race reached its climax, Lily's team found themselves neck and neck with another group. The final challenge involved a giant slip-and-slide that led to a finish line marked by a banner of confetti.

Lily took a deep breath, her heart racing with a mix of excitement and adrenaline. With a running start, she launched herself onto the slippery surface and slid down, her laughter echoing through the air as she sailed toward the finish line.

The moment she crossed the banner, confetti exploded around her, and the cheers of the crowd enveloped her in a wave of exuberance. Lily's team had won the race, but more importantly, they had won the opportunity to share in a day filled with laughter and connection.

As the festivities continued, Lily couldn't help but appreciate the way Mooington had once again brought people together in the spirit of fun and camaraderie. The Whimsical Race was a reminder that even in the midst of life's challenges, there was always room for a good laugh and a dash of whimsy.

Chapter 22: The Unusual Discovery

The laughter and jubilation from the Whimsical Race had left an indelible mark on Mooington. The town seemed to radiate an energy that was equal parts joy and camaraderie, an enchantment that had brought people together in the most delightful ways.

Lily found herself wandering through the town's charming streets, her heart light and her thoughts filled with the memories of the day's festivities. As she passed by the town's clock tower, a glimmer of curiosity tugged at her.

A group of townspeople had gathered around the clock tower, their expressions a mix of awe and excitement. Lily approached them, her curiosity getting the better of her.

"What's going on?" she asked one of the onlookers.

A woman turned to her with a wide grin. "We've just discovered something truly unusual—something that has the town buzzing with excitement!"

Intrigued, Lily joined the group, her eyes widening at the sight before her. An intricately designed contraption had been uncovered beneath the clock tower. Gears, cogs, and a series of levers adorned the contraption, creating a mesmerizing display of mechanical artistry.

Isaac, the town's beloved storyteller, stood at the center of the crowd, his eyes gleaming with intrigue. "Ladies and gentlemen, whimsical beings, and seekers of the extraordinary, feast your eyes on the Unusual Discovery—a marvel of engineering and wonder!"

Lily marveled at the contraption's intricate details, her fascination growing with each passing moment. It seemed that Mooington had yet another surprise in store, a testament to the town's ability to blend magic and innovation.

As the crowd whispered with anticipation, Isaac explained that the contraption was a collaborative creation—a fusion of Mooington's enchantment and the talents of the town's inventors and tinkerers. It was designed to bring delight and surprise to the town, a whimsical addition to the enchantment that already filled the air.

With a theatrical flourish, Isaac pulled a lever, setting the contraption in motion. Gears began to turn, levers moved, and a series of colorful flags unfurled, creating a symphony of movement and color.

The crowd burst into applause and cheers, their excitement palpable. Lily watched as children clapped their hands in delight and adults exchanged knowing glances, united in their appreciation for the unexpected treasure that had been uncovered.

As the contraption continued its mesmerizing dance, Lily felt a sense of awe wash over her. The Unusual Discovery was a reminder that Mooington's magic was not confined to the realm of enchantment—it extended to the realm of creativity and innovation as well.

As the day turned into evening, Lily found herself standing beside Bessie, the flying cow, who mooed softly as if in approval of the newfound wonder. The town's clock tower, once a symbol of time's passage, had now become a beacon of imagination and whimsy.

Chapter 23: A Comical Conundrum

In the midst of Mooington's enchantment, Lily's thoughts often turned to Gabriel. The memory of his unexpected disappearance weighed heavily on her heart, but she was determined to find a way to rescue him from whatever whimsical twist of fate had spirited him away.

One day, as the sun painted the sky with hues of gold and rose, Lily found herself in the town square, lost in thought. Bessie, the flying cow, playfully tugged at her sleeve as if urging her to take action.

"You're right, Bessie," Lily mused, giving the cow's fluffy wings a pat. "I can't just sit around and hope for a solution. I need to take matters into my own hands."

With newfound determination, Lily embarked on a quest of her own. She visited the town's eccentric inventor, Mr. McWidget, whose workshop was a treasure trove of contraptions and whimsical devices.

"Ah, Lily my dear, what brings you here?" Mr. McWidget greeted her with a twinkle in his eye, his monocle wobbling precariously on his nose.

Lily explained her predicament to the inventor, her voice a mix of earnestness and desperation. "I need to find a way to rescue Gabriel from wherever he's ended up. Do you have any inventions that could help?"

Mr. McWidget scratched his chin thoughtfully, a contraption of gears and springs whirring to life beside him. "Rescuing a missing person, you say? Hmm, I might just have the thing!"

He led Lily to a curious contraption that looked like a mix between an oversized umbrella and a pogo stick. "Behold, the Res-Q-Brella! With this marvel of ingenuity, you can bounce your way through dimensions and timelines."

Lily couldn't help but raise an eyebrow at the contraption's absurd appearance. "Are you sure this will work?"

Mr. McWidget grinned, his mustache twitching. "Well, there's only one way to find out, isn't there?"

With a mixture of apprehension and determination, Lily gripped the Res-Q-Brella's handle and gave it a tentative bounce. To her surprise, the contraption sprung to life, propelling her into the air with a comical boing.

As Lily soared through the sky, she couldn't help but laugh at the sheer absurdity of her situation. She bounced over rooftops, sailed through clouds, and even did a loop-de-loop that left her stomach in knots.

Finally, with a final bounce, Lily landed in a place that was unlike any she had ever seen before. It was a world of swirling colors, upside-down trees, and talking animals with top hats.

As she looked around in bewilderment, a familiar voice sounded from behind her. "Lily, is that you?"

Lily's heart leaped as she turned to see none other than Gabriel standing before her, a mix of surprise and amusement in his eyes.

"Gabriel!" Lily exclaimed, rushing to embrace him. "I've been searching for you everywhere!"

Gabriel chuckled, his eyes crinkling with mirth. "Well, it seems you've found me in the most unexpected of places."

As they caught up on their respective adventures, Lily couldn't help but shake her head in disbelief. The Res-Q-Brella had indeed worked, but not in the way she had expected. It had brought her to a dimension of whimsical absurdity, where reality itself seemed to have taken a comical twist.

Chapter 24: The Chuckle Dimension

Lily and Gabriel stood in the topsy-turvy world of swirling colors and comical landscapes. It was a realm where gravity seemed to have a playful sense of humor, trees sported mustaches, and giggles echoed through the air like music.

"I can't believe this place," Lily said, her laughter mingling with the strange sounds of the dimension. "It's like we've stepped into a cartoon!"

Gabriel nodded, his eyes sparkling with amusement. "It's definitely unlike anything I've ever experienced."

As they explored the Chuckle Dimension, as they had come to call it, Lily and Gabriel encountered all manner of absurdities. They crossed bridges made of rubber chickens, rode on merry-go-rounds that spun in every direction at once, and even engaged in conversations with sentient clouds that told jokes.

"I must say, this place really takes the idea of 'laughing until your sides hurt' to a whole new level," Gabriel remarked as they stumbled upon a field of bouncing flowers that released bursts of confetti with every bounce.

Lily couldn't help but laugh as she plucked a confetti-filled petal and twirled it in the air. "It's like the Chuckle Dimension is determined to keep us in stitches!"

As they continued their comical exploration, Lily and Gabriel found themselves in the company of the dimension's peculiar inhabitants—a group of sentient balloons that communicated through melodious squeaks and rubbery gestures.

"We've been expecting you," one of the balloons squeaked, its voice surprisingly melodious.

Lily exchanged a glance with Gabriel, her curiosity piqued. "Expecting us? How did you know we'd be here?"

The balloon stretched its rubbery body in what appeared to be a shrug. "The laughter in the air told us. Your arrival was foretold by the mirthful winds."

Gabriel raised an eyebrow, his lips twitching with a smile. "Well, I suppose that's one way to be welcomed."

As they conversed with the balloon inhabitants, Lily and Gabriel learned that the Chuckle Dimension was a place born from the sheer joy of laughter and the boundless creativity of Mooington's enchantment. It was a realm that existed outside the bounds of time and space, a whimsical haven where the rules of reality were merely a suggestion.

"We're here to seek answers," Lily said, her voice filled with earnestness. "We need to know how to get back to our own world."

The balloons bobbed and swayed, their squeaks taking on a contemplative tone. "The way back is paved with laughter, but it's a path you must discover on your own."

Gabriel exchanged a glance with Lily, and they both knew what they had to do. They began to share stories, jokes, and anecdotes, their laughter filling the air as they recounted their adventures and experiences. The Chuckle Dimension responded in kind, its landscapes shifting and changing with each burst of laughter.

Hours passed in a whirlwind of giggles and guffaws, until finally, the dimension itself seemed to respond to the abundance of joy. The swirling colors intensified, and Lily and Gabriel felt a sensation of weightlessness.

With a burst of light, they found themselves back in Mooington's town square. The enchanting landscapes of the Chuckle Dimension had given way to the familiar charm of their own world.

Lily and Gabriel looked at each other, their hearts still light from the laughter-filled journey. "We did it," Lily said, her voice a mix of wonder and relief. "We found our way back."

Gabriel grinned, his eyes dancing with mirth. "And we did it with the power of laughter."

As they stood amidst the enchantment of Mooington, Lily and Gabriel knew that their bond had been strengthened by the comical adventure they had shared. The Chuckle Dimension had shown them that even in the most unexpected places, laughter had the power to guide them back to where they belonged.

Chapter 25: A Tale to Remember

As Lily and Gabriel stood in the heart of Mooington, their laughter-filled adventure in the Chuckle Dimension behind them, they felt a deep sense of gratitude for the town's enchantment and the bond they had forged through whimsy and camaraderie.

The town square buzzed with activity, townsfolk going about their daily routines, and the enchantment that had brought Lily and Gabriel together in the first place. Bessie, the flying cow, gave a contented moo as if to acknowledge their return.

"We've been through quite the journey, haven't we?" Gabriel mused, his eyes filled with a mix of fondness and amusement.

Lily nodded, a smile tugging at her lips. "From the mysteries of disappearing people to the laughter-filled antics of the Chuckle Dimension, it's been an adventure I'll never forget."

Gabriel's gaze softened as he looked at Lily. "And I couldn't have asked for a better companion to share it with."

Their laughter, their shared moments of whimsy, and the challenges they had faced together had deepened their connection in ways they hadn't anticipated. Mooington's enchantment had woven its magic not only around the town itself but also around the hearts of those who had experienced its wonder.

As the sun set over the charming town, casting a warm glow over its cobblestone streets, Lily and Gabriel found themselves in a place of quiet reflection. They had journeyed through the realms of mystery, comedy, and enchantment, emerging stronger and more connected than ever before.

"We'll always have these memories," Lily said softly, her gaze drifting to the clock tower that stood as a sentinel of time's passage.

Gabriel nodded, his voice gentle. "And the magic of Mooington will forever be a part of us."

As they stood together, Lily and Gabriel knew that the story of their time in Mooington would be one they would carry with them for the rest of their lives. The laughter, the camaraderie, and the enchantment they had experienced had transformed their lives in ways they could never have imagined.

Don't miss out!

Visit the website below and you can sign up to receive emails whenever Jaime Orozco publishes a new book. There's no charge and no obligation.

https://books2read.com/r/B-A-MFXZ-DXRMC

BOOKS 2 READ

Connecting independent readers to independent writers.

Did you love *Cows are Flying*? Then you should read *THE LAST MAN ON EARTH*[1] by Jaime Orozco!

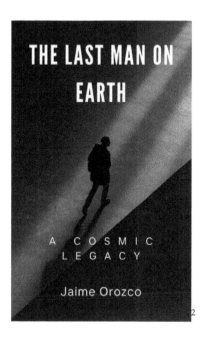

"The Last Man On Earth" follows the journey of an astrophysicist who wakes up to find himself alone in the world. With humanity mysteriously vanished, he becomes the celestial guardian, tasked with protecting the delicate balance of the universe. As he traverses the cosmos, he encounters celestial wonders, confronts enigmatic forces, and discovers the profound interconnectedness of all life. Guided by memories of his past and the souls of the vanished, he embarks on an epic odyssey of love, unity, and the eternal dance of existence. This cosmic tale celebrates the enduring legacy of humanity and the timeless beauty of life's celestial symphony.

---

1. https://books2read.com/u/b6GjAE

2. https://books2read.com/u/b6GjAE

Also by Jaime Orozco

Le Dragon Malicieux
Les Gardiens de la Forêt
Missing star in the universe
Sombras del Pasado
THE LAST MAN ON EARTH
Cows are Flying
Gazing Upward - Opening the Cosmic Curtain
Le Monstre Jaune
Lemonade and Dinosaurs
The Fearless Little Bird

About the Author

I am a passionate author drawn to the world of literature, constantly seeking new horizons in writing. My creativity overflows onto every page, inviting readers to an exciting journey through imaginary worlds and unforgettable characters. Each written word is an expression of my love for stories and the desire to inspire others through them.

Milton Keynes UK
Ingram Content Group UK Ltd.
UKHW010001240823
427351UK00001B/91